Twins Have a Fight

By Ellen Weiss
Illustrated by Sam Williams

ALADDIN
New York London Toronto Sydney

First Aladdin edition June 2004

ALADDIN PAPERBACKS
An imprint of Simon & Schuster Children's Publishing Division
1230 Avenue of the Americas
New York, NY 10020

Book design by Debra Sfetsios
The text of this book was set in Century Oldstyle.

Printed in the United States of America
2 4 6 8 10 9 7 5 3 1

Library of Congress Cataloging-in-Publication Data

Weiss, Ellen, 1949–
Twins have a fight / by Ellen Weiss ; illustrated by Sam Williams.—
1st Aladdin pbk. ed.
p. cm. — (Ready-to-read)
Summary: Rhyming text follows a set of twins as they fight over two new
toys, break one, and learn to share the other.
ISBN 0-689-86515-5 (pbk. : alk. paper) — ISBN 0-689-86516-3 (lib
edition)
[1. Fighting (Psychology)—Fiction. 2. Sharing—Fiction. 3.
Twins—Fiction. 4. Stories in rhyme.] I. Williams, Sam, 1955– ill. II.
Title. III. Series.
PZ8.3.W4245Tu 2004
[E]—dc21
2003011611

What is in the box?

Can it be socks?

Two new toys!

Happiness! Joy!

Mine is blue.

The green is for you.

The blue one is mine!

Do not whine.

I got it first.

You are the worst!

Give it to me!

Let me see!

Do not grab.

Do not be a crab!

Do not take it!

You will break it!

Uh-oh.

Now we have one.

Sharing is fun!